This edition published by Parragon Books Ltd in 2014 and distributed by

Parragon Inc.
440 Park Avenue South, 13th Floor
New York, NY 10016
www.parragon.com

ISBN 978-1-4723-7845-3

Printed in China

Cinderella's
Book of
Secrets

PaRRagon
Bath · New York · Cologne · Melbourne · Delhi
Hong Kong · Shenzhen · Singapore · Amsterdam

This book belongs to

_____

Contents

All about you 8

Pretty pictures 10

Sweet secrets 12

Loyal friends 14

Friend photographs 16

Beautiful birthdays 18

Princess party 20

My family 22

Animal friends 24

Sweet dream diary 26

Magical music 28

Perfect plans 30

My special year 32

Things to do 44

All about you

Cinderella wants to know all about you,
especially your special secrets!
Fill them in on these pages.

Name: ....

Nickname: ....

Hair color: ....

Eye color: ....

Birthday: ....

Age: ....

Lucky number: ....

Best friends: ....

....

....

....

Favorite animal: ....

Favorite color: ....

Favorite season: ....

Favorite flower: ....

Best talent: ....

Worst habit: ....

The thing I'm most proud of: ....

....

....

....

Happiest moment: ....

....

....

....

....

Pretty pictures

Have an adult help you cut out some of your favorite
photographs, and glue them onto these pages.
Cinderella has included a picture of her best
friends, the mice, and a special party.

Me as a baby

My best friend

A party!

The mice

Me on vacation

My favorite thing

My family

Sweet secrets

All your secrets are safe with Cinderella!

My biggest secret:

....

....

....

....

....

My secret wish for this year:

....

....

....

....

....

A secret I want to tell somebody:

....

....

....

....

A secret I have already shared:

....

....

....

....

My secret dream when I grow up:

....

....

....

....

Loyal friends

Cinderella's friends are very important to her. The mice are always ready to help when she needs them. Who are your best friends? Write about them on these pages.

Name: ....

Hair color: ....

Eye color: ....

Their best talent: ....

....

What I like about them: ....

....

....

Name: ....

Hair color: ....

Eye color: ....

Their best talent: ....

....

What I like about them: ....

....

....

Name: ....

Hair color: ....

Eye color: ....

Their best talent: ....

....

What I like about them: ....

....

....

Friend photographs

Fill these pages with your favorite photographs of your friends!

Beautiful birthdays

A loyal friend never forgets a birthday. Fill in your friends' and relatives' birthdays on these pages.

Name: ....

Birthday: ....

Age this year: ....

Gift ideas: ....

....

Name: ....

Birthday: ....

Age this year: ....

Gift ideas: ....

....

Name: ....

Birthday: ....

Age this year: ....

Gift ideas: ....

....

Name: ....

Birthday: ....

Age this year: ....

Gift ideas: ....

....

Name: ....

Birthday: ....

Age this year: ....

Gift ideas: ....

....

Princess party

Cinderella loves to throw parties for her friends and the Prince. Use these pages to plan your own princess party! Cinderella has added some of her own ideas to help you.

Guest list:...

....

....

....

....

....

....

Party food and drinks:

Pink and blue cupcakes
....
....
....
....
....
....
....

Party music:

....
....
....
....
....
....
....
....

What games will you play?

Musical statues!
....
....
....
....

My family

Cinderella hasn't always gotten along with her stepmother and stepsisters. What is your family like? Write about it on these pages.

Who is the funniest? ....

Who makes the most mess? ....

Who is good at helping out? ....

Who takes care of everyone? ....

How would your family describe you?

....

....

....

....

....

....

Stick your favorite family

photograph here!

Animal friends

Cinderella's best friends are mice, but she loves other animals too. What pet do you have? If you don't have one, fill in these pages for your dream pet.

Type of animal: ....

Name: ....

Age: ....

Fur or body color: ....

Eye color: ....

Best trick: ....

Favorite food: ....

The thing I like best about them: ....

....

....

....

....

....

Stick a photograph
of your pet here!

Sweet dream diary

When Cinderella lived with her cruel stepmother, she often dreamed of a happier life. What do you dream about? Write your dreams here so you can remember them later.

Date: ....

Describe the dream: ....

How did you feel when you woke up?

....

....

....

....

What do you think it meant? ....

....

....

....

Date: ....

Describe the dream: ....

....

....

How did you feel when you woke up? ....

....

What do you think it meant? ....

....

Date: ....

Describe the dream: ....

....

....

How did you feel when you woke up? ....

....

What do you think it meant? ....

....

Magical music

Cinderella and the mice love to dance to beautiful music. What music do you like?

Who is your favorite singer or group? ....

....

Which song always makes you want to dance? ....

....

Which instruments can you play? If none, which would

you like to learn? ....

....

What would you call your group?..

....

....

Use this page to write some words that could be turned into a song. Try to use rhyming words like "dance" and "chance".

Perfect plans

Every princess has dreams and wishes for the future.
What are yours? Try to imagine yourself in ten years' time.

How old will
you be?

....

Where will you be living?

....

What will you do
each day?

....

....

....

....

Where will you go
on vacation?

....

Who will you live with?

....

....

Who will be your
best friend, and why?

....

....

....

....

....

....

Draw a picture of what you think you'll look like in the future.

January

My favorite thing about January:

....

....

....

Birthdays that
were in January:

....

....

....

....

....

....

The best thing
I did this month:

....

....

....

....

....

Favorite animal
moment this month:

....

....

....

....

In January, the weather was:

....

February

My favorite thing about February:

....

....

....

The best thing I did this month:

....

....

....

....

....

Birthdays that were in February:

....

....

....

....

....

....

....

Favorite thing my best friend did this month:

....

....

....

....

In February, the weather was:

....

March

My favorite thing about March:

....

....

....

Birthdays that were in March:

....

....

....

....

....

....

....

The best thing I did this month:

....

....

....

....

....

....

The best dream I had in March:

....

....

....

In March, the weather was:

....

April

My favorite thing about April:

....

....

....

Birthdays that were in April:

....

....

....

....

....

....

The best thing I did this month:

....

....

....

....

....

Something new I learned in April:

....

....

....

In April, the weather was:

....

May

My favorite thing about May:

....
....
....

The best thing
I did this month:

....
....
....
....
....
....

In May, the weather was:

....

Birthdays that
were in May:

....
....
....
....
....
....
....

A secret wish
I made in May:

....
....
....

June

My favorite thing about June:

....

....

....

The best thing
I did this month:

....

....

....

....

....

....

In June, the weather was:

....

Birthdays that
were in June:

....

....

....

....

....

....

A new treasure
I found in June:

....

....

....

....

July

My favorite thing about July:

....

....

....

**The best thing
I did this month:**

....

....

....

....

....

....

In July, the weather was:

....

**Birthdays that
were in July:**

....

....

....

....

....

....

**A new friend
I made in July:**

....

....

....

August

My favorite thing about August:

....
....
....

Birthdays that were in August:

....
....
....
....
....
....
....

The best thing I did this month:

....
....
....
....
....
....

A new favorite place I found:

....
....
....

In August, the weather was:

....

September

My favorite thing about September:

....

....

....

Birthdays that were in September:

....

....

....

....

....

....

The best thing I did this month:

....

....

....

....

....

The best place I visited:

....

....

....

In September, the weather was:

....

October

My favorite thing about October:

....

....

....

**The best thing
I did this month:**

....

....

....

....

....

In October, the weather was:

....

**Birthdays that
were in October:**

....

....

....

....

....

....

....

**Something new I
wish for the future:**

....

....

....

November

My favorite thing about November:

....

....

....

**The best thing
I did this month:**

....

....

....

....

....

....

In November, the weather was:

....

**Birthdays that
were in November:**

....

....

....

....

....

....

....

**My favorite
family moment:**

....

....

December

My favorite thing about December:

....

....

....

The best thing I did this month:

....

....

....

....

....

....

Birthdays that were in December:

....

....

....

....

....

....

....

....

My wish for the new year:

....

....

....

In December, the weather was:

....

Things to do

Cinderella has found her true love and is happily living in the royal palace, but she still has hopes and dreams for the future. What is on your to-do list? Perhaps you'd like to learn an instrument or visit a particular place?

To do: ....

....

Target date: ....

To do: ....

....

Target date: ....

To do: ....

....

Target date: ....

To do: ....

....

Target date: ....

To do: ....

....

Target date: ....

To do: ....

....

Target date: ....

To do: ....

....

Target date: ....

To do: ....

....

Target date: ....